P9-EGN-524

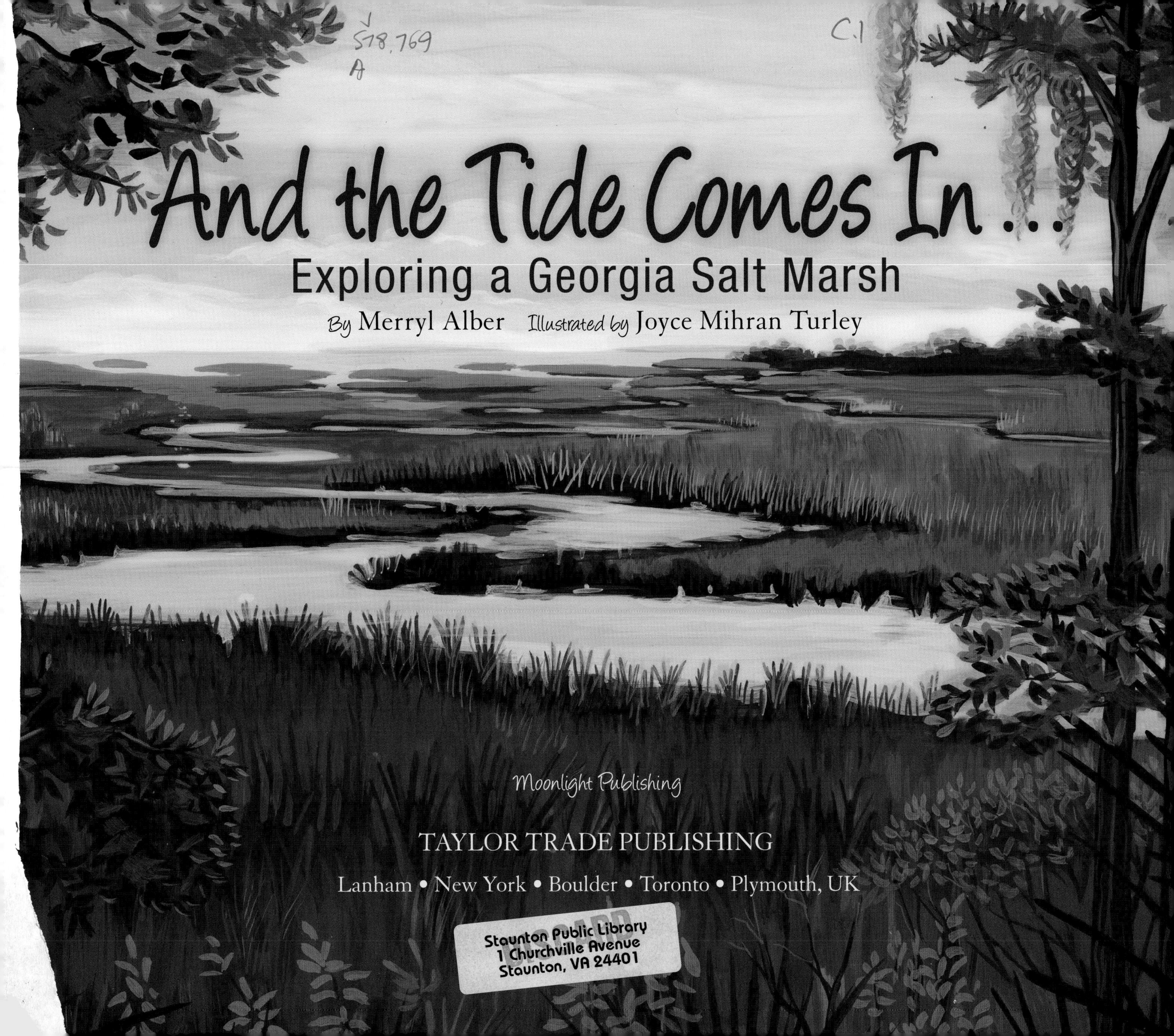

And the Tide Comes In . . .

Exploring a Georgia Salt Marsh

By Merryl Alber Illustrated by Joyce Mihran Turley

Moonlight Publishing

TAYLOR TRADE PUBLISHING

Lanham • New York • Boulder • Toronto • Plymouth, UK

Published by
Taylor Trade Publishing

An imprint of
The Rowman & Littlefield Publishing Group, Inc.
4501 Forbes Boulevard, Suite 200, Lanham, Maryland 20706
www.rowman.com

Estover Road, Plymouth PL6 7PY, United Kingdom

Distributed by National Book Network

British Library Cataloguing in Publication Information Available

Library of Congress Cataloging-in-Publication Data Available

ISBN 978-0-9817700-5-5 (cloth)

ISBN 978-0-9817700-7-9 (electronic)

Printed in Malaysia

About the Long Term Ecological Research (LTER) Network (lternet.edu)

The LTER network is a large-scale program supported by the National Science Foundation. It consists of 25 ecological research projects, each of which is focused on a different ecosystem. The goals of the LTER network are:

Understanding: To understand a diverse array of ecosystems at multiple spatial and temporal scales.

Synthesis: To create general knowledge through long-term, interdisciplinary research, synthesis of information, and development of theory.

Information: To inform the LTER and broader scientific community by creating well designed and well documented databases.

Legacies: To create a legacy of well designed and documented long-term observations, experiments, and archives of samples and specimens for future generations.

Education: To promote training, teaching, and l earning about long-term ecological research and the Earth's ecosystems, and to educate a new generation of scientists.

Outreach: To reach out to the broader scientific community, natural resource managers, policymakers, and the general public by providing decision support, information, recommendations, and the knowledge and capability to address complex environmental challenges.

Acknowledgements

This book is part of the Long Term Ecological Research (LTER) program Schoolyard Series, which seeks to engage children and their families in learning about the earth's ecosystems (schoolyard.lternet.edu). Financial support came from National Science Foundation awards to the Georgia Coastal Ecosystems (GCE) LTER project and to the LTER book fund. Scientists at the GCE LTER provided technical review, and participants in the GCE Schoolyard program developed lesson plans and connection questions. We thank Diane McKnight, Amy and Rick Rinehart, and Taylor Trade for their support throughout this effort.

Dedication

For Brian, Barrett, and "the gang." —M.A.

For my brothers Greg and Rick, with whom I spent long summer days flooding the sandpile to make mud, catching tadpoles in the pond, and rolling down the grassy hills in our yard. —J.M.T.

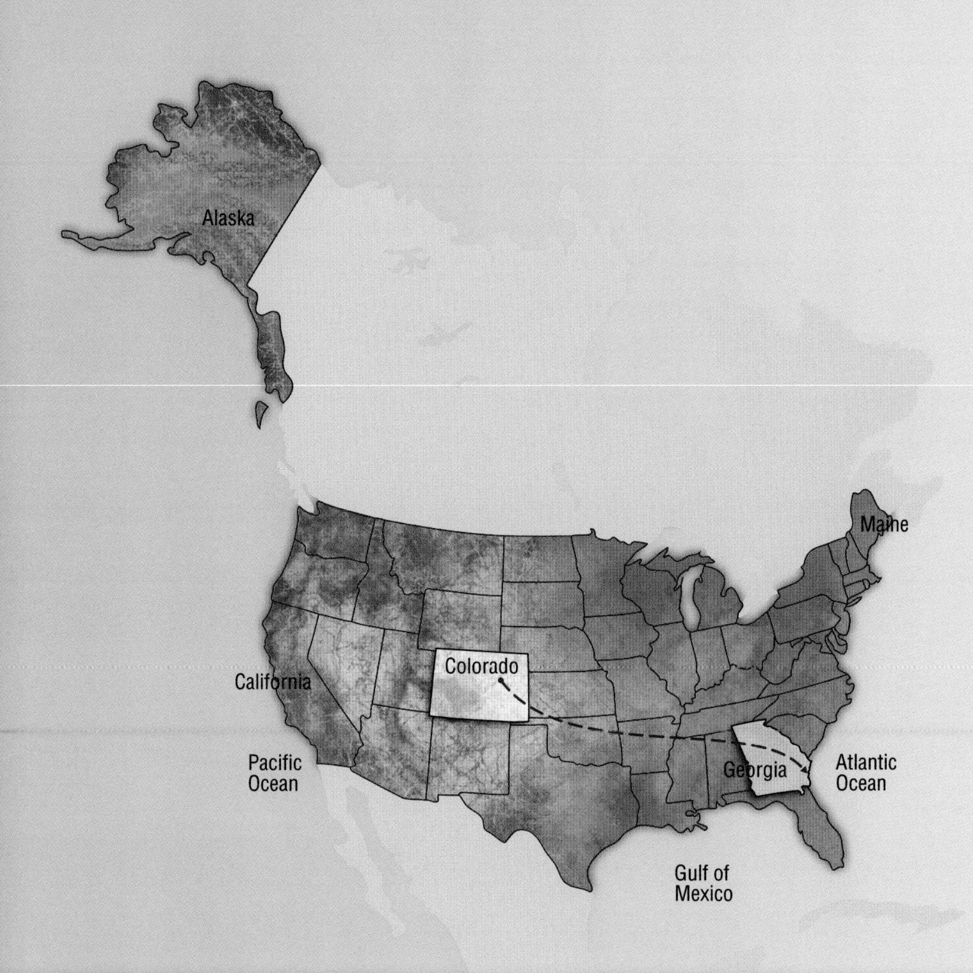

The United States is bordered by two different oceans: the Pacific Ocean, which reaches from Alaska to Southern California in the west, and the Atlantic Ocean, which reaches from Maine to Florida in the east. The Gulf of Mexico, which runs from Texas to the tip of Florida, also drains to the Atlantic Ocean.

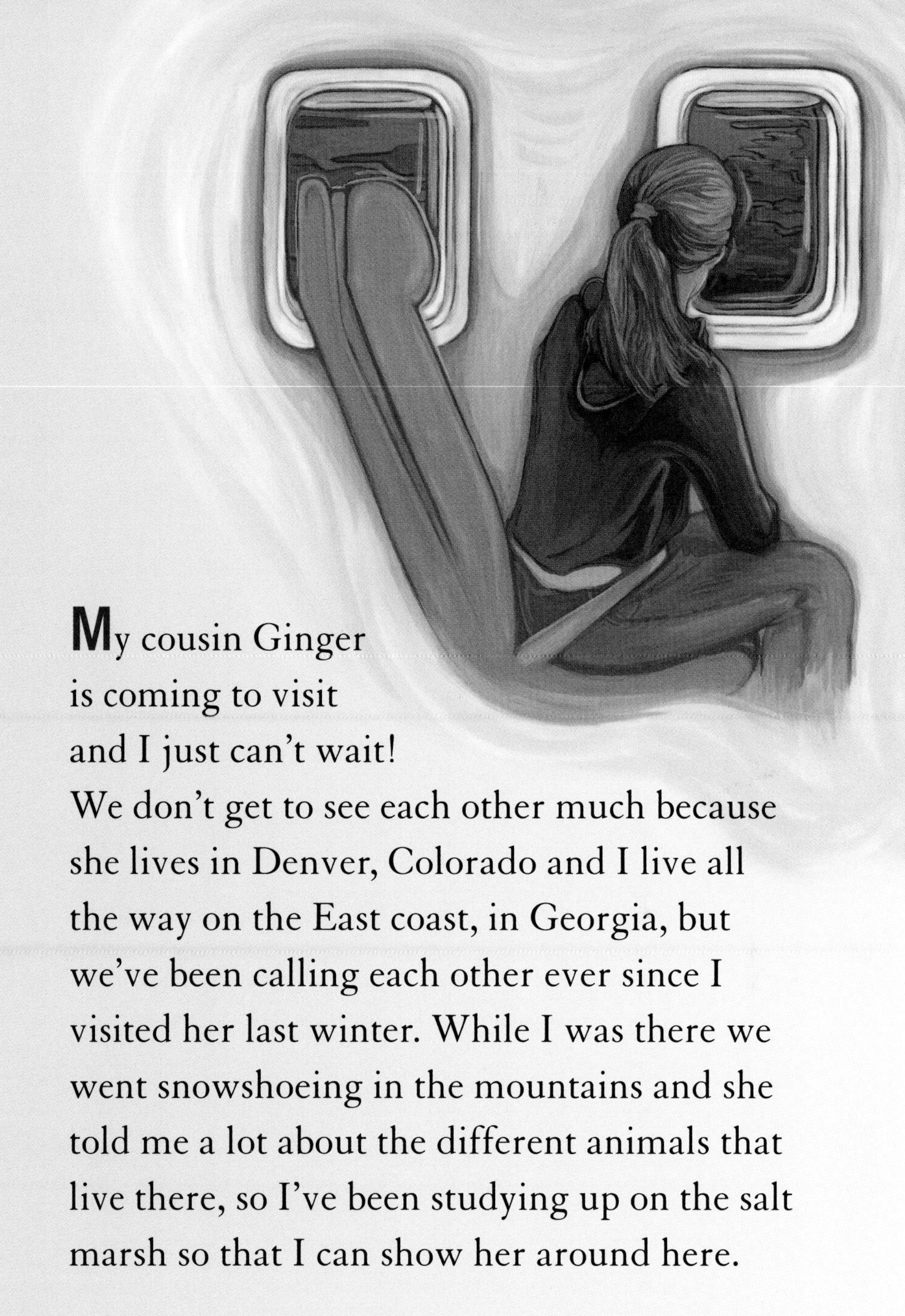

My cousin Ginger is coming to visit and I just can't wait! We don't get to see each other much because she lives in Denver, Colorado and I live all the way on the East coast, in Georgia, but we've been calling each other ever since I visited her last winter. While I was there we went snowshoeing in the mountains and she told me a lot about the different animals that live there, so I've been studying up on the salt marsh so that I can show her around here.

Which ocean is the closest to where you live?

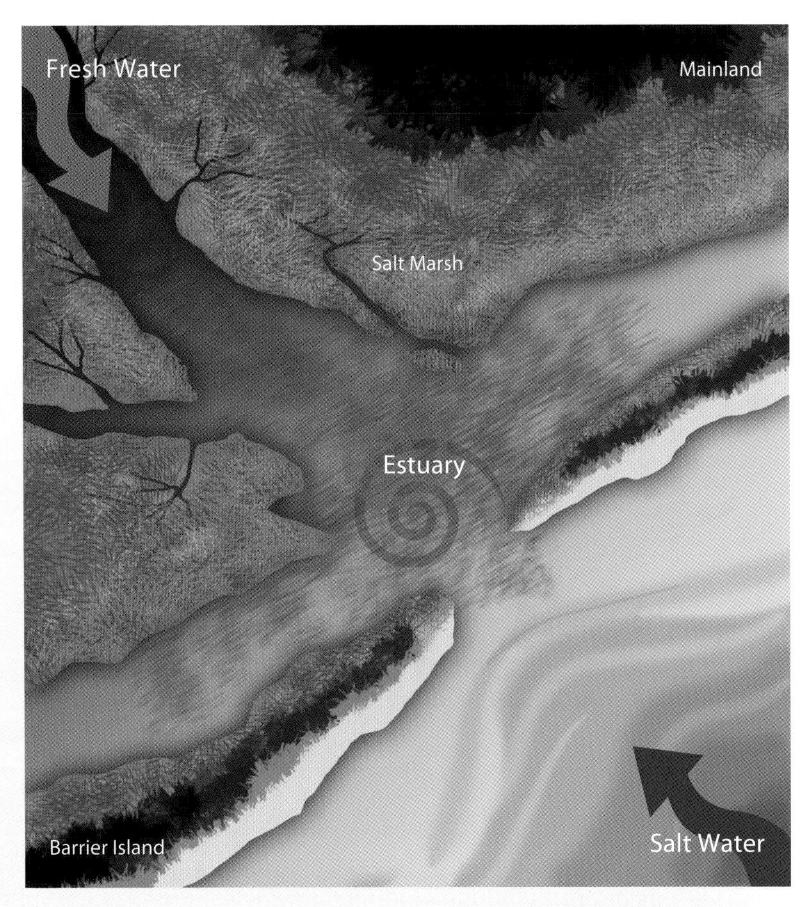

Estuaries are places where salt water from the ocean mixes with fresh water from the land. Salt marshes are found in protected areas such as the edges of estuaries and the back sides of coastal islands. Because marshes are on the edge of the land, one of the things they do is help shelter coastal areas from storms. When there are big waves, like during a hurricane, they get spread though the marshes, which provide protection for people's houses. Salt marshes are found all over the world; most of the ones in the US occur on the East and Gulf coasts.

On the way home from the airport our parents are talking up a storm, but Ginger is pretty quiet. When we pull into my driveway, she turns to me and says "I thought you lived on the coast." "I do!" I say. "But where's the sand? Where are the waves?" "Oh, you mean the beach. We can go to the beach, but the marsh is much closer. You see, beaches are on the outside edge of the land, but the salt water from the ocean reaches miles and miles inland as it comes up the river. The ocean brings water to us every day, and then it takes it away." "And the marsh?" she asks. "The marsh? The marsh is in between! Let's get you settled in and then I'll show you."

Have you ever been in a big storm?

What helped to protect you?

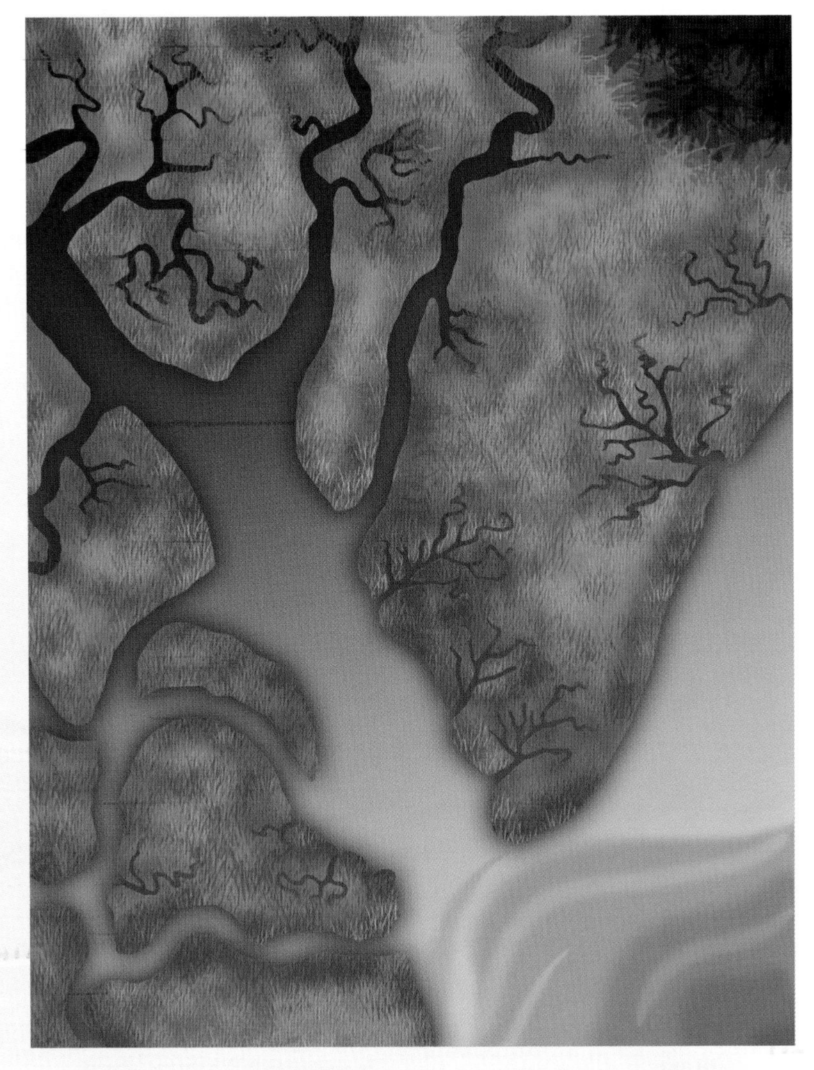

Tidal creeks are small creeks that are filled with salty water and come right up into the marsh. Wider creeks give way to smaller and smaller creeks as you get closer to the upland. At low tide the creek's edges are pretty easy to see, but at high tide the water overflows onto the surrounding marsh land.

Mom says we can go to the marsh for just a little while before dinner. I give Ginger some of my marsh clothes and a pair of my old sneakers. She asks me why she has to wear such messy-looking things, and all I can say is "you'll see." We take the trail that leads through the woods behind my house, and after awhile the marsh comes into view. It's summer so the marsh grass is pretty tall: it always reminds me of an overgrown lawn of yellowy-green hay. We also get a good view of the creek as it winds its way through the marsh and out to the main part of the river, connected like the branch of a tree.

Is there a creek near your home?
Do you know where it goes?

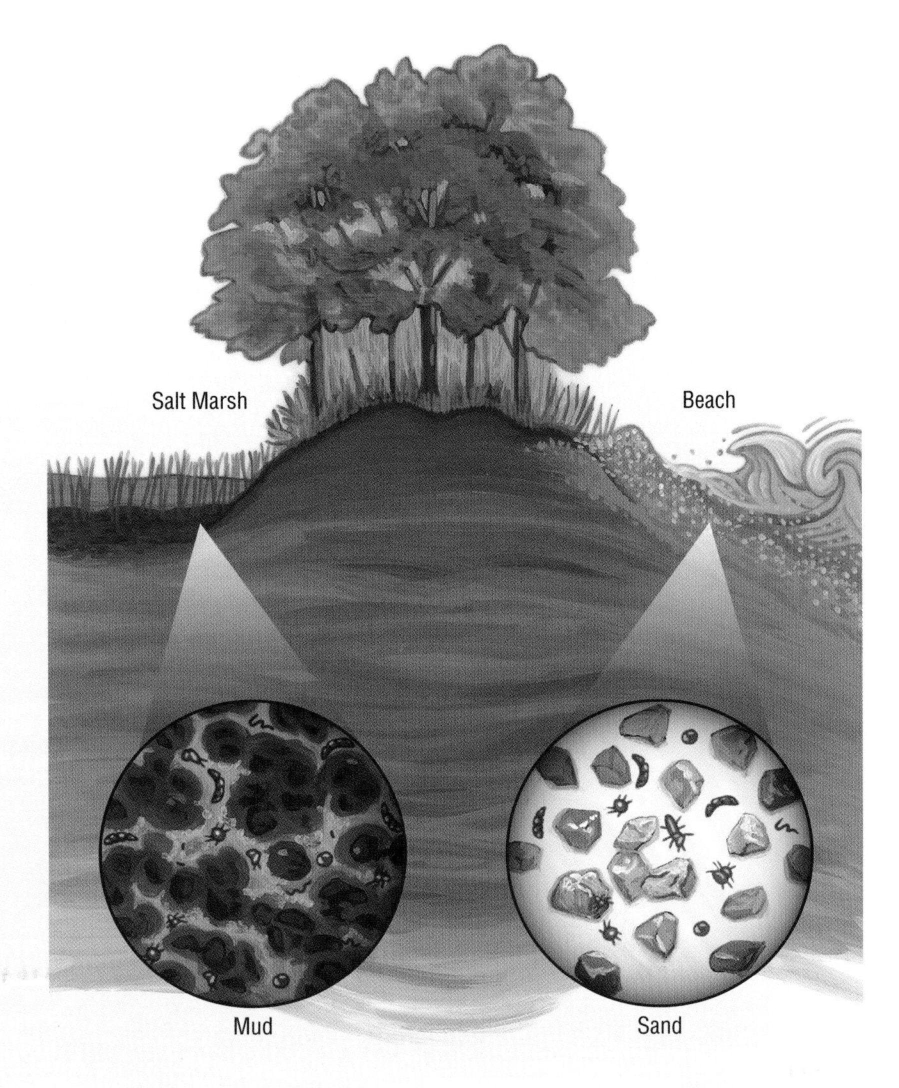

Marshes are muddy because the water flows in gently, without large waves. In contrast, beaches are sandy because the waves can carry sand, which weighs a lot more than mud. The marsh mud is full of small organisms and dead plant material, which are important in providing food and energy for the rest of the marsh.

When we reach the edge of the woods, I pause, but Ginger walks right out into the grass. “Wait!” I say. Too late. Ginger has already started to slide and before I know it she slips down into the mud, right at the edge of the creek. “That’s why I wear old clothes” I say, “marshes are muddy.” “Now you tell me” Ginger laughs. She’s having a little trouble getting up, so I get a piece of driftwood and use it to help pull her up. When she’s upright again she plants the driftwood into the grass and says, “This will mark the spot where I first found out about marsh mud.”

Have you ever gotten really muddy? What did you do to get clean?

Salt marsh plants are pretty tough, because they get flooded with salt water and that would kill most plants. Many of the plants that are found in marshes have special adaptations for making sure that they don't get too salty. One trick, which is used by salt marsh cord grass, is to keep the fresh water inside the leaves and move the salt crystals to the outside.

I want to tell Ginger about the marsh plants and how they get watered with salt water, but she's more interested in the animals. I point out a clump of mussels near the base of the marsh grass. "These are ribbed mussels. They're hard to pull up because they attach to things with tiny little hairs," I say, tugging at a mussel to show her. There are so many things to see that Ginger can't stay still. "What's this?" she asks, picking up a small white snail from the stem of a plant. "That's a periwinkle" I say. "Hold your hand still for a minute." At first nothing happens, but then the snail comes slowly out of its shell and starts to crawl around. As we quietly watch it exploring her hand, I hear a familiar clicking sound. "Do you hear that noise?" I ask.

Can you think of some foods that have salt crystals on the outside?

Ginger nods as I point to all of the fiddler crabs skittering around on the edge of the creek. I scoop one up and hold it out to show her. (I'm pretty good at catching them; my Dad showed me how to hold them so they can't pinch.) "See all these holes everywhere? Those are fiddler crab burrows." Ginger is interested in the crab, but she doesn't want to hold it. "I'll stick with snails" she says. There are so many things I want to show her, but it's getting late and we need to head back. "Plus, it's going to take a while to get me cleaned up!" jokes Ginger, pointing to the mud all over her pants.

Tides are caused by the pull of gravity from the Moon (and a little bit from the Sun) on the Earth's oceans, which makes the water "bulge" on the side closest to the Moon, where gravity is strongest. Water also bulges away from the Moon on the opposite side of the Earth, where gravity is weakest and does not pull the water very much. Since the Earth is rotating, high tides occur when a particular spot is under a bulge, and low tides when it's in between them. In most places, there are two high tides and two low tides every day, which means the tide changes about every 6 hours.

The next morning Ginger wants to get started as early as possible. "We're Marshians!" we tell our parents. "Not the kind from outer space — the kind that explores marshes!" We head down the trail, and Ginger is way out ahead of me. When we get to the edge she stops in surprise. "The marsh is gone!" she exclaims. "We better go back and tell everyone the water's rising and there's sure to be a flood!" I'm laughing so hard I can't stop. Ginger looks kind of mad but then I tell her that the marsh is still there. "It's just that it's high tide and it's under water. The water comes up from the ocean, and all the way back up here to the marsh." I point to the piece of driftwood, which we can just see sticking up out of the water. "The tide will go out again after a few hours and you'll be able to see the ground again. It goes in and out, twice a day."

Can you describe the movement of the Moon and the Earth?

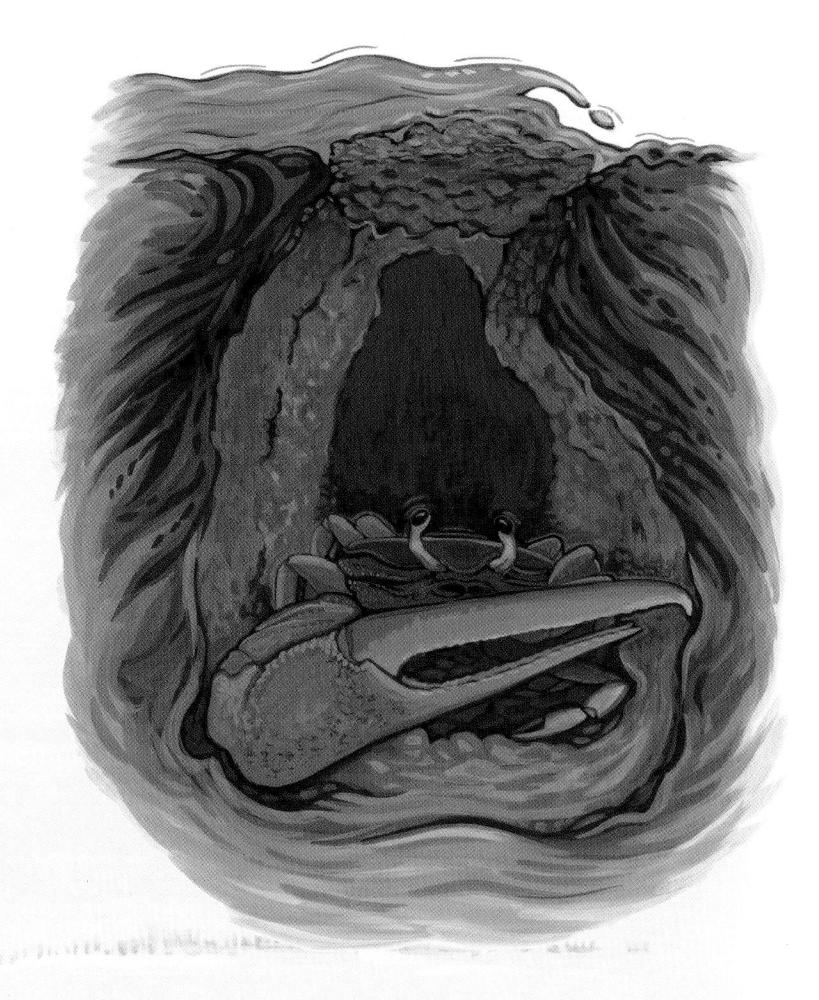

Fiddler crabs breathe air. During high tide, they go down into their burrows and plug the hole with mud. One mystery is how they know when it is low tide again, so that it is safe to open the hole and come back up onto the marsh. Scientists think the crabs have a special "clock" that lets them know what the tide is doing. It is easy to tell male and female fiddler crabs apart because the males have one claw that's much larger than the other, which they sometimes wave around.

"But where are the snails?" she asks. "The snails are still here — look, they've just climbed up the grass." She looks around, and sure enough the snails can be found clinging to the tips of the plants. "And the crabs?" she asks. "The crabs are hiding in their burrows. They go into them as the tide comes in." "How long do they have to stay down there?" "Well, until the tide goes out again." "So all of the animals just have to hold their breaths and wait for the water to go away?" she asks. "Well, not exactly. There are oysters that live on the edge of the creek, and at low tide they close up and wait for the water to come back. Now that they're covered they're able to filter their food from the water." We stand for awhile. I'm used to the tides, but after explaining it to Ginger I realize how amazing it is that the water on the marsh right now will flow back into the creek, out to the river and all the way to the ocean.

How might you tell time without a clock?

Raccoons are usually thought of as nocturnal animals, which sleep during the day and come out at night to feed. In marshes though, especially in isolated areas, raccoons come out during low tide to feed, regardless of whether it is day or night. Other mammals that use the marsh include deer, bobcats, marsh rice rats, and mink.

Later that afternoon we head back down the path. Ginger sounded like an expert when we left the house, telling her parents that it's low tide now so we'll be able to get out onto the marsh. As I come out of the woods I freeze and motion for Ginger to be quiet. She comes up slowly beside me and gasps. Not far from the driftwood marker there's a raccoon digging up the mussels! It sees us though and quickly scurries away. "Wow" I say. "I see their footprints a lot but I hardly ever see raccoons." "It ran back to the woods" says Ginger. "Yes" I say, "there are lots of animals from the woods that come down at low tide to feed on the marsh, just the same as there are fish and turtles in the water that come in at high tide." "So they share the marsh," she says. "That's pretty cool!"

What animals have you seen visiting your neighborhood?

Blue crabs are born in the ocean, but they grow up in the estuary. Young blue crabs can be found in shallow water, and they come up on the marsh at high tide. As blue crabs grow they molt, which means that they shed their shells when they get too small. Sometimes the crab's discarded shells can be found in the salt marsh, and scientists think that they hide in the grass to protect themselves from predators when they molt.

Out in the distance we hear the chug chug of a motor, and a small boat appears. We watch as it slowly moves through the water toward a red float bobbing on the surface. "What's that boat doing?" asks Ginger. "Oh, that's a crabber. The float is attached to his trap." We can see the trap glittering in the sunlight as the crabber pulls it into the boat. "You mean, people catch fiddler crabs way out there?" she says, pointing to the holes at our feet. "No" I laugh, "he's catching blue crabs. You won't find fiddler crabs out there, and I don't know anybody who eats them anyway. Blue crabs do come up into the marsh though. Remember how we saw the snails up out of the water at high tide? That's a way for them to escape from being eaten by the blue crabs." "Speaking of eating, I'm getting hungry" says Ginger. "So am I" I tell her. "Plus, I think we're going out to dinner tonight!"

How often do you outgrow your clothes?

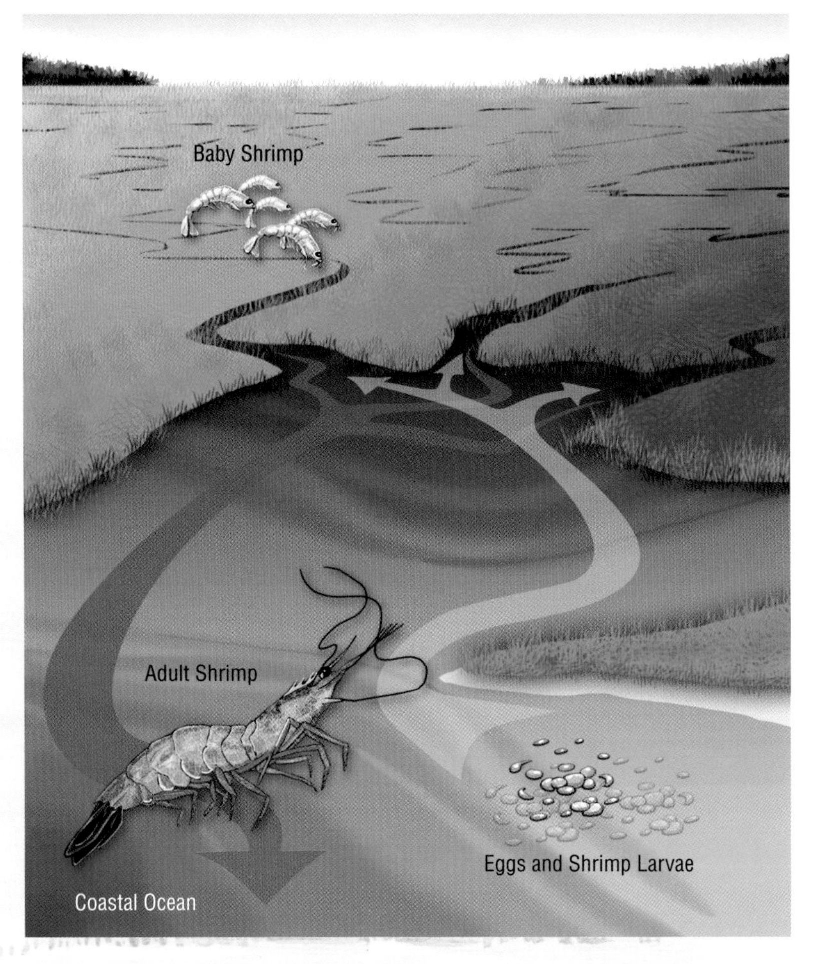

Just like crabs, shrimp are born in the ocean but grow up in the estuary. Because they can get so much good food in the marsh, there are more shrimp in areas with more marshland. When the shrimp reach adult size, they turn around and swim back out to the ocean. The adult female lays her eggs in the ocean, and the cycle starts all over again.

All the way to Captain Scott's, Ginger is telling her parents about the animals we saw. When her Dad orders crab cakes, she tells him about the blue crabs and how they come into the marsh to feed. We both order shrimp cocktail, and my Mom says "Now, you know girls, those shrimp spend time in the marsh too." "They do?" I say. "I thought the shrimp boats went out into the ocean." "You're right, the shrimp boats don't come up the river" says Mom, "but the baby shrimp are in the creeks, and then, when the tide comes in…" "they swim up into the marsh!" says Ginger, before Mom can finish her sentence. "That's right" laughs Mom. "And I bet they're eating while they're up there" continues Ginger. "Well, yes, they are, but they also hide in the marsh grass so they don't get eaten themselves. It's pretty hard for a big fish to follow them through all that grass." "Like hide and seek" says Ginger. "Exactly" Mom smiles.

Can you think of other animals that look different when they are born?

Georgi
LIVE OAK

Most of the animals that live in the marsh release their eggs into the water, where they hatch into larvae. The eggs and larvae are part of the plankton, which are living organisms that drift along with the currents. If they're lucky, the larvae settle down in the marsh, where they grow into adults, remaining on land for the rest of their lives.

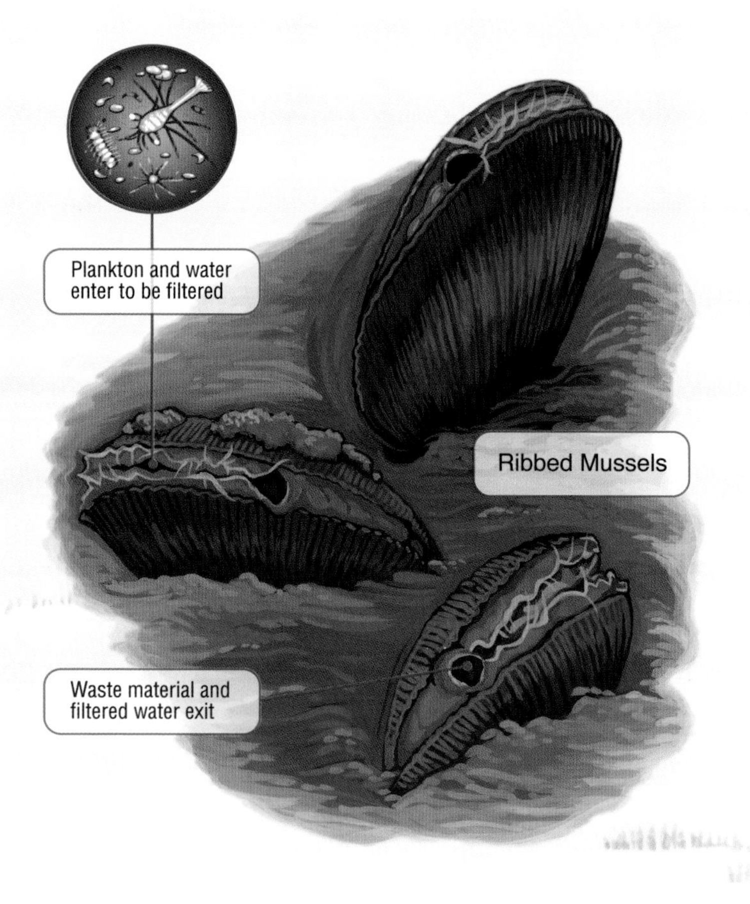

The next day we decide to wait until after lunch before heading out to the marsh, since low tide isn't until 3:00. When we get there the water is just leaving. "Come look, I want to show you something" I say. I carefully peel away a brown leaf from the stem of a piece of marsh grass, and pick out a tiny shell. "Oh my gosh — it's a little bitty snail, isn't it?" "Yep, and it'll grow to be one of these" I say, pointing towards an adult periwinkle. "But how did it get in there? Is that where the mother laid its eggs?" asks Ginger. "Nope" I say. "The eggs go off into the water." "They do? But then that means they go out with the tide!" "That's right, but remember, the tide comes back too. So when the babies are ready to settle down, the lucky ones get brought back to the marsh and settle on a plant." "The lucky ones?" she says. "Well, the ones that don't make it end up as fish food! But enough of them manage to get here, as you can see," I say, pointing at the snails around us.

What have you seen floating in the water?

Lots of birds can be seen in salt marshes, flying overhead, pecking for food in the mud, or fishing from the edge of a creek. Some, like clapper rails and marsh hawks, build their nests in the marsh and are there all the time. Others, like egrets, roost in nearby trees. Still others, like ring-billed gulls, pass through on their way south for the winter. You can think of the marsh as a neighborhood coffee shop, with local birds that are there every day and others from farther away that just stop by for a visit.

"This place is amazing" says Ginger. "If we see an animal in the marsh, it might have come from the land, like the raccoon, or it might live in the marsh as an adult but in the water as a baby, like the snail."
"Or, it might come from the air!" I say, pointing to a marsh hawk circling in the distance. On our way back through the grass a grasshopper jumps out and hits my backpack. "Another land animal using the marsh" laughs Ginger.

Where have you seen birds eating?
Have you seen their nests?

It’s Ginger’s last day so we get up early to visit the marsh one more time. The tide is rising so we can’t get out to the driftwood. We walk as far as we can and then stand and watch as the water comes towards us. “I’m going to miss this place” says Ginger. “We never did make it to the beach” I say. “I know” she smiles, “but we did get good and muddy!” We both laugh. “Promise you’ll call” she says. “I will” I say. We’re both quiet. The water is grey today, and it merges with the sky. After a while we turn to leave, and the tide comes in.

The salt marsh described in this book is on the coast of Georgia, but marshes are found in intertidal areas all over the world. As long as the area is protected, the slope of the land is gentle, and there are some freezing temperatures, there is likely to be a marsh. (In warm, tropical areas that never get cold enough to freeze, mangroves are found in protected, gently sloping areas.) All salt marshes are covered by salty water brought in from the ocean during high tide, and exposed to the air during low tide. Although the particular plants and animals found in marshes do differ from one area to another, they are all shared by land and marine animals, and they're all covered with grasses that can withstand getting flooded by salt water. And remember, if you get the chance to visit a marsh, be sure to wear old clothes!

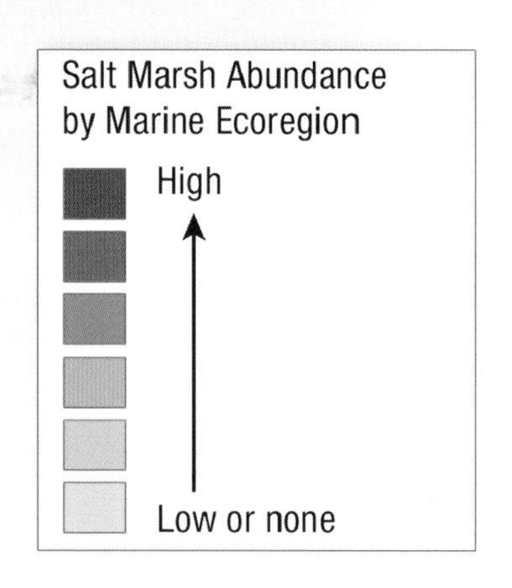

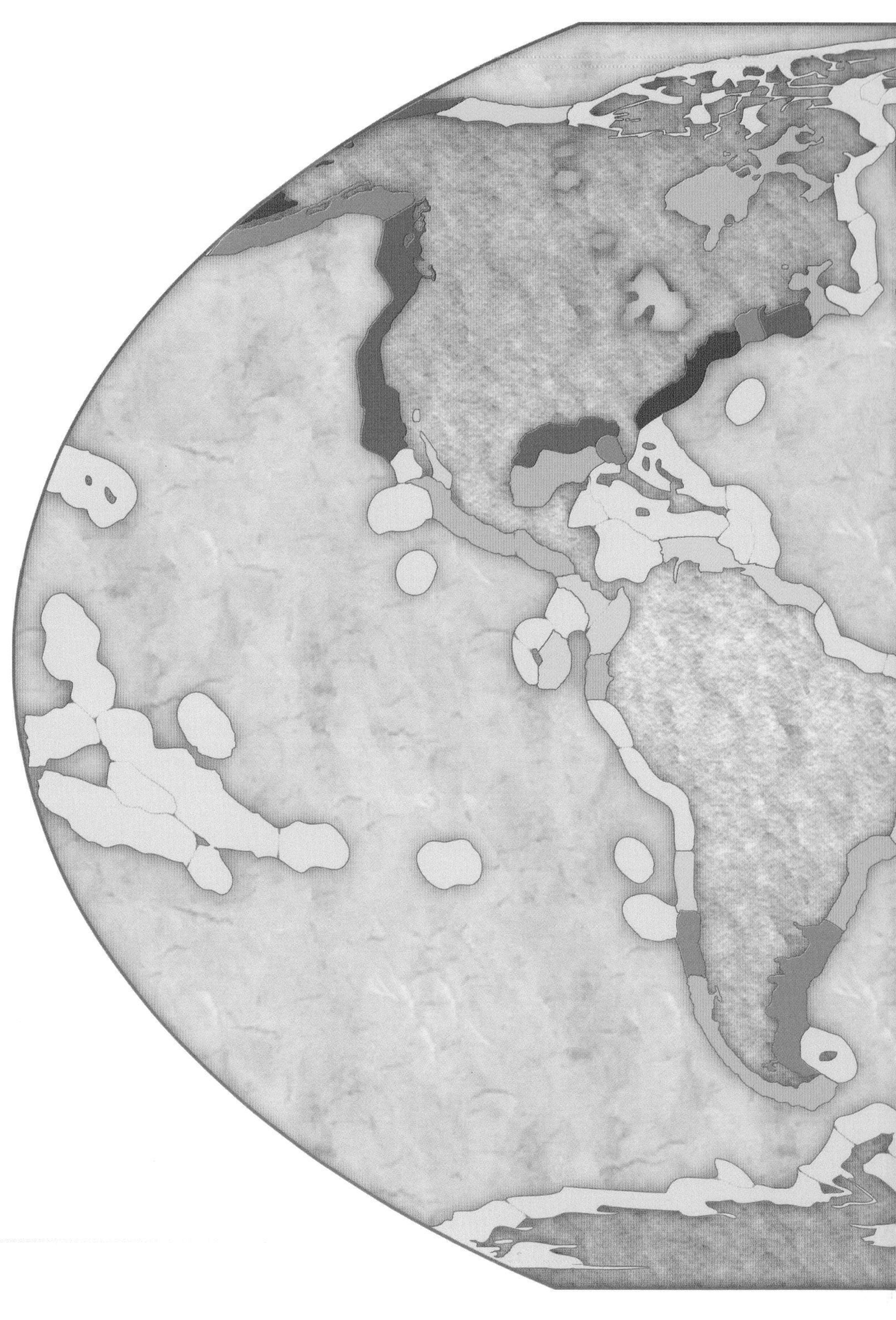

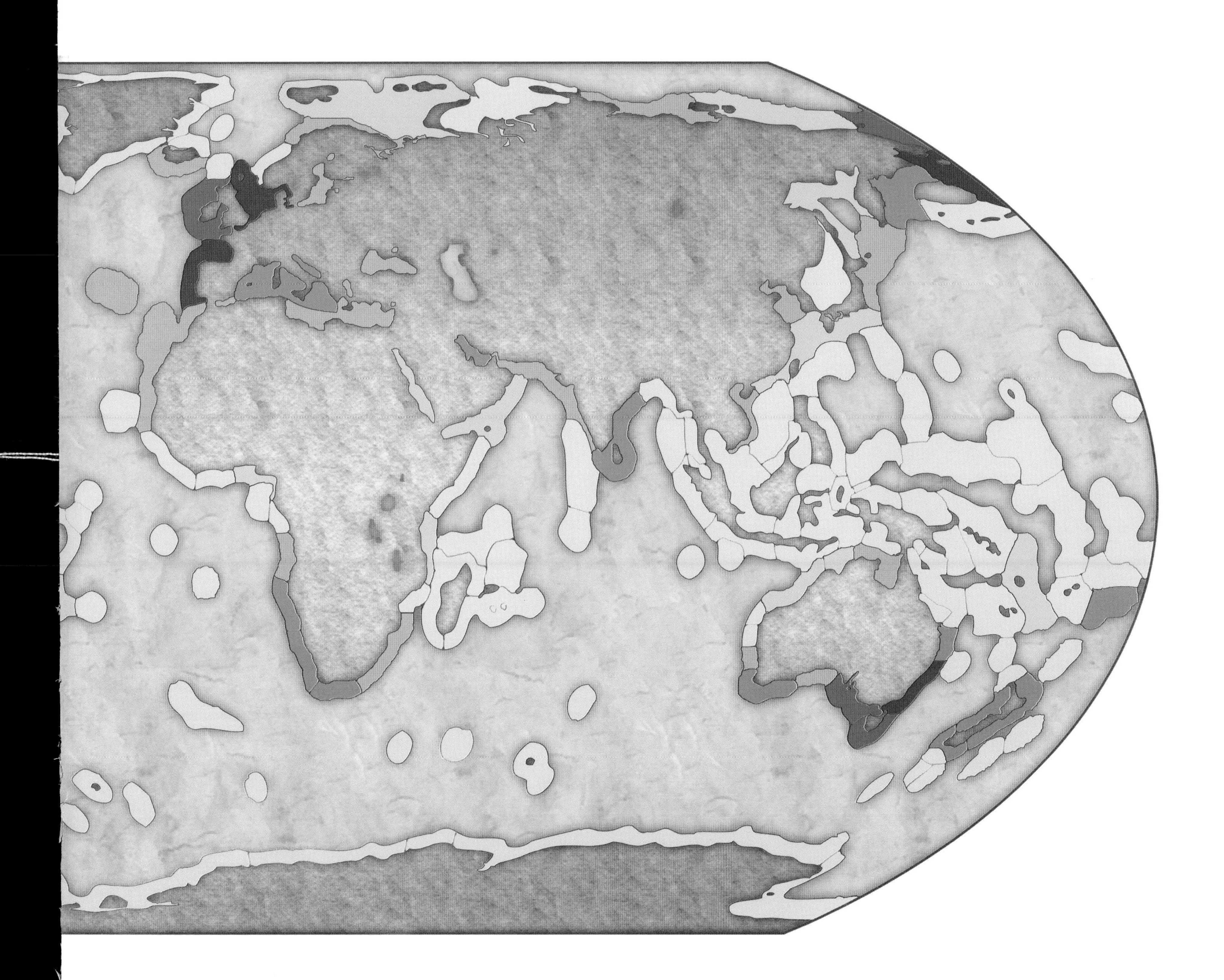

About the Author and Illustrator

Photo credit: Barrett Binder

Merryl Alber is a Professor in the Dept. of Marine Sciences at the University of Georgia who directs the Georgia Coastal Ecosystems Long Term Ecological Research program. She is a marine ecologist who has conducted research in salt marshes in both the southeastern and northeastern U.S. Dr. Alber holds a B.S. from Duke University and a Ph.D. from the Boston University Marine Program. She lives in Athens, GA, with her husband and their teenage son.

Photo credit: Rick Turley

Joyce Mihran Turley specializes in presenting images of nature with a painterly style and colorful palette, engaging readers of all ages. Her recent works focus on introducing children to the native animals and unique ecosystems of our national parks including Everglades, Grand Canyon, and Glacier. Her bird illustrations appear in award-winning nonfiction books for children. Having studied mathematics along with fine art, Joyce retired from engineering over 25 years ago to pursue her interest in illustration. Her technical perspective results in vibrant illustrations with a unique balance of analytic and artistic elements. Raised in upstate New York, Joyce has lived with her husband in the foothills of the Colorado Rockies for over 30 years. Her studio, located in their now "empty nest," permits convenient observation of deer, coyotes, lizards, eagles, and snakes—just outside the picture windows!

About GCE LTER

The Georgia Coastal Ecosystems LTER (gce-lter.marsci.uga.edu/) is one of 25 NSF-sponsored LTER sites. Scientists involved in the GCE LTER project study the marshes and estuaries of the Georgia coast in order to understand how these ecosystems function, to track how they change over time, and to predict how they might be affected by future variations in climate and human activities.

If you would like to learn more about marshes please visit us at gce-schoolyard.uga.edu, where you will find supplementary materials and lesson plans as well as drawings, essays, and other materials submitted by children who have read this book. The website also has information about the GCE LTER Schoolyard program and provides access to data collected by GCE scientists, a species list, a bibliography, and links to other resources.